MW01268141

502586

WORLD'S BEST SOLDIERS

SPECIAL FORCES: PROTECTING, BUILDING, TEACHING, AND FIGHTING

AIR FORCE

ARMY RANGERS

ELITE FORCES SELECTION

ESCAPE AND EVASION

GREEN BERETS

MARINES

NAVY SEALS

URBAN WARFARE

PARACHUTE REGIMENT

WORLD'S BEST SOLDIERS

WORLD'S BEST SOLDIERS

by C. F. Earl

Mason Crest Publishers

MASON CREST PUBLISHERS INC.
370 Reed Road
Broomall, Pennsylvania 19008
(866)MCP-BOOK (toll free)
www.masoncrest.com

First Printing
9 8 7 6 5 4 3 2 1

Library of Congress Cataloging-in-Publication Data

Earl, C. F.
 The world's best soldiers / by C.F. Earl. – 1st ed.
     p. cm.
 Includes bibliographical references and index.
 ISBN 978-1-4222-1846-4 ISBN (series) 978-1-4222-1836-5
 1. Special forces (Military science)—Juvenile literature. I. Title.
 U262.E17 2011
 356'.16—dc22
                        2010024705

Produced by Harding House Publishing Service, Inc.
www.hardinghousepages.com
Interior design by MK Bassett-Harvey.
Cover design by Torque Advertising Design.
Printed in USA.

With thanks and appreciation to the U.S. Military for the use of information, text, and images.

Contents

Introduction

Elite forces are the tip of Freedom's spear. These small, special units are universally the first to engage, whether on reconnaissance missions into denied territory for larger conventional forces or in direct action, surgical operations, preemptive strikes, retaliatory action, and hostage rescues. They lead the way in today's war on terrorism, the war on drugs, the war on transnational unrest, and in humanitarian operations as well as nation building. When large-scale warfare erupts, they offer theater commanders a wide variety of unique, unconventional options.

Most such units are regionally oriented, acclimated to the culture and conversant in the languages of the areas where they operate. Since they deploy to those areas regularly, often for combined training exercises with indigenous forces, these elite units also serve as peacetime "global scouts," and "diplomacy multipliers," beacons of hope for the democratic aspirations of oppressed peoples all over the globe.

Elite forces are truly "quiet professionals": their actions speak louder than words. They are self-motivated, self-confidant, versatile, seasoned, mature individuals who rely on teamwork more than daring-do. Unfortunately, theirs is dangerous work. Since the 1980 attempt to rescue hostages from the U.S. embassy in Tehran, American special operations forces have suffered casualties in real-world operations at close to fifteen times the rate of U.S. conventional forces. By the very nature of the challenges that face special operations forces, training for these elite units has proven even more hazardous.

Thus it's with special pride that I join you in saluting the brave men who volunteer to serve in and support these magnificent units and who face such difficult challenges ahead.

—Colonel John T. Carney, Jr., USAF–Ret.
President, Special Operations Warrior Foundation

CHAPTER 1

Elite Units in History

Commanders throughout history have sought to create within their armies special units that could shatter an opponent's troops in battle, However, as the nature of warfare has changed, so has the role of elite forces.

Elite fighting units are not a new idea. Throughout history, armies have contained units that have received superior training, equipment, and experience. Persia's Immortals, Alexander the Great's Companion Cavalry, Renaissance Switzerland's Pikeman, Napoleon's Imperial Guard, and Britain's Guards Regiments are all clearly entitled to their elite status. Although separated by thousands of years, they

UNDERSTAND THE FULL MEANING

elite: The best of a group.

have something in common: they are battle-winning forces. Their very dependability, their willingness to remain steadfast under heavy fire before then launching attacks to punch their way through an enemy's lines, made them a valuable **asset** to any commander. Napoleon fully appreciated the potential of his Guard units, often keeping them in reserve until the enemy had been fixed in position and battered by his more expendable line units.

The nineteenth century, however, saw a change in the makeup of the elite forces. Previously, elites had fought as a regular part of an army on the battlefield. But during the 1800s, they began to be used more as specialists who could fight in an **unconventional** way. The British had used bands of skilled woodsmen, such as Rogers' Rangers, to take on the French and native tribes in North America in the mid-eighteenth century. They were later forced to create units of special **infantry** to deal with enemy sharpshooters in the American Revolutionary War (1775–1783). In contrast to previous elites, these forces consisted of highly skilled individuals who were allowed to fight independently and display individual initiative in combat. Similar units, which were equipped with rifles, accompanied the Duke of Wellington's army in the Peninsular Campaign in Spain (1808–1814).

UNDERSTAND THE FULL MEANING

asset: A good thing to have, which will help accomplish what is needed.

unconventional: Unusual, not the normal way of acting or doing something.

infantry: Soldiers who fight on foot.

The New Hampshire Sharpshooters were known for the accuracy of their shooting. They formed one of the earliest elite forces within the U.S. Military.

Colonel John S. Mosby served the American Special Forces between 1860 and 1865.

Yet to many European military leaders, these special units seemed an "ungentlemanly" way to conduct war. It was America that took the idea of elite soldiers to the next level. The American Civil War (1861–1865) saw the emergence of elites that had more in common with Rogers' Rangers than Napoleon's Imperial Guard. The U.S. First Infantry Regiment, better known as Berdan's Sharpshooters, did not fight as regular infantry. Instead, they fought as individuals or in small groups. Their role was to shoot at enemy officers or other important targets. Marksmanship, together with accurate long-range rifled muskets, was what marked them out as elite. Meanwhile, the South's Confederacy created a number of "raiding" forces, under men such as John Mosby and Nathan Bedford Forrest. These mounted units were lightly equipped and operated away from the main Southern armies. They struck at will against weak points of the North's army and supply routes.

The lessons of the American Civil War took a long time to be learned in Europe. However, wartime experience, particularly for the British, soon brought about a big change of mind. The Boer War saw the British outmaneuvered and outshot by mobile Afrikaans farmers. Columns of British and Commonwealth infantry and cavalry slogged across the African plains after an elusive enemy. This was an enemy that fought from trenches and used accurate, aimed shots to cut down rank after rank of slow-moving British units as they marched across the open terrain. Losses, particularly in Black Week (when the British lost three battles), forced the British Army to think again about elites.

In response, the British sent what were called Imperial Yeomanry units. These units were made up mostly of men from Australia, New Zealand, and Canada. Mounted on horseback and lightly equipped, their ranks were filled with hardy and skilled frontiersman who were often the equal of the Boers in marksmanship. The yeomanry chased and harried the Boers as never before and undoubtedly helped in their defeat. This experience was of great importance to the British Army, and they took the lessons learned into World War I (1914–1918).

Yet the idea of individual initiative was still very much discouraged. It was the Imperial German Army in the latter stages of the war that created the first truly elite units (at least in the modern sense). Operation "Michael," the last-ditch attempt to cut through the Allied lines in 1918, saw the large-scale use of elite soldiers called "Stormtroopers." These units were filled with expertly trained veterans. Stormtroopers went into battle in small units, carrying lots of weapons. Unlike regular units, which were supposed to capture large pieces of enemy ground, their role was to find weaknesses in the enemy line and smash through quickly and ruthlessly, The Stormtroopers would then push deep behind enemy lines to create confusion.

Though Germany did not win World War I, it had learned how useful elite soldiers could be. It used elite soldiers even more in World War II (1939–1945). The defeat of France and her allies in the summer of 1940 was helped along by a handful of special forces. Highly trained bands of paratroopers were used to capture a massive Allied fort in Belgium.

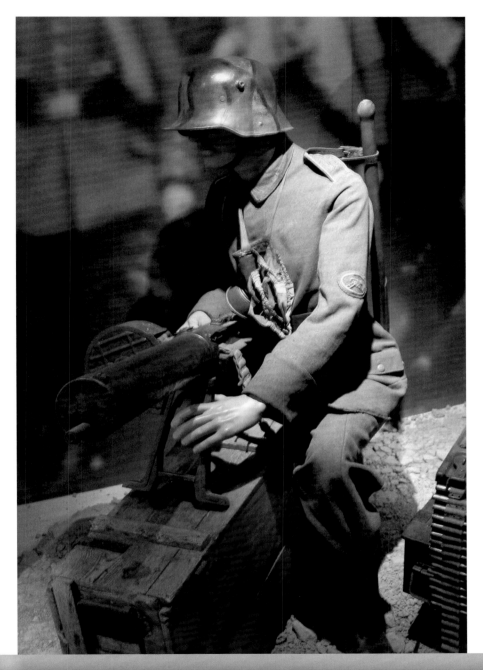

This museum recreation shows a German Stormtrooper, an elite soldier trained to push deep into enemy territory.

Elite German troops seized a railway bridge in Holland by disguising themselves as Dutch military police. Later in the war, German units were involved in a variety of what are now seen as classic examples of elite-force missions. They rescued the Italian dictator Benito Mussolini from his mountaintop prison at Gran Sasso in Italy. They also used English-speaking Brandenburger units to sabotage bridges behind enemy lines in late 1944.

If Germany led the way in the field of elite forces, Britain and the United States were not far behind. In Britain, thanks in part to the enthusiasm of Prime Minister Winston Churchill, many large and small units were raised to strike back into occupied Europe. Army and Royal Marine Commandos, paratroopers, and a variety of specialized naval units launched dozens of raids against the French coastline. In North Africa, the Special Air Service Regiment (SAS) helped to undermine the German and Italian ability to fight by hitting targets behind the front line. Units raised in the United States, such as the Rangers and paratroopers, went on to play vital roles in the invasions of North Africa, Italy, France, and Germany. They also contributed to victory in the Pacific.

The end of World War II saw many elite forces disbanded. However, they were soon needed again. After World War II, there were many countries within the colonies of Britain, France, and Portugal that suddenly tried to overthrow their rulers. This meant that many small wars occurred in Africa and Asia. What were required were units schooled in the

SAS troops in France during World War II.

arts of **guerrilla** warfare, units capable of meeting the enemy on their own terms.

Specialized training was developed in such areas as weapons, survival skills, communications, and medicine. Britain's SAS showed the value of this training during missions in places such as Malaya, Borneo, Aden, and Oman. The U.S. Special Forces were specifically created to cope with Viet Cong guerrillas in Vietnam by winning the confidence of local tribesman and turning them into a fighting force.

More recently, special forces have been faced with a new type of war known as terrorism, the worst cases of which were the attacks on New York and Washington, D.C., on September 11, 2001, which claimed many thousands of lives. Elite units such as the Special Air Service, Germany's GSG 9, and France's GIGN have been created to fight these terrorist forces.

Today's elite forces are taught many different skills. They learn to carry out raids, to conduct hostage-rescue missions, and, above all, to operate in small groups, often behind enemy lines. As the 1991 Gulf War demonstrated, these units can have an amazing effect.

In this book, we will look at some of the world's best units. There is not space here to look at them all, so we have picked different units around the world to see why they are

UNDERSTAND THE FULL MEANING

guerrilla: Having to do with fighting tactics such as surprise raids, ambushes, and sabotage.

What Recruiters Look for in Elite Solders

Selection courses for elite units are the toughest military training in the world. Candidates must possess stronger qualities than the average soldier. This is what the recruiting officers look for in a recruit:

- **endurance**

  Can you keep going even when your body and mind are exhausted?

- **intelligence**

  Can you solve difficult problems when they arise, even when you are under great stress and pressure?

- **team spirit**

  Are you wiling to put the well-being of the team above your own needs?

- **self-control**

  Are you able to control your emotions and think clearly when you are under pressure?

- **sense of humor**

  If you cannot laugh when bad things happen, will you become worried or depressed under stress?

the best. They are of very different sizes. The U.S. Airborne Forces, for example, have many thousands of soldiers, while the Australian SAS is a small organization. However, each elite unit is among the best of the world's soldiers.

CHAPTER 2
U.S. Airborne Forces

The American 82nd and 101st Airborne Divisions are some of the most highly trained and best-equipped forces in the world. As the Gulf War in 1991 proved, they are masters of the modern battlefield.

The first man to come up with the concept for U.S. Army parachute forces was General "Billy" Mitchell. He suggested it as early as 1918, but because many other generals were old-fashioned, the idea was quickly dropped. However, Germany and the Soviet Union started to develop their own parachute battalions after the war, watched closely by Britain and America. So, in 1939, the U.S. Chief of Infantry suggested the creation of an American parachute formation.

In 1940, the 501st Parachute Infantry Battalion was created. At first, there were not many aircraft and parachutes to go around. But more parachute battalions quickly followed. In 1942, the famous 82nd "All American" and 101st

"Screaming Eagles: Airborne Divisions" were formed. These large airborne units also had airborne artillery and engineers, as well as infantry regiments that could land by special military gliders.

American paratroopers made their first parachute jump into combat in North Africa in November 1942. A few months later, the airborne soldiers made more combat parachute jumps into Sicily and southern Italy. By the time Italy surrendered in September 1943, the American and British paras were experienced in this new form of warfare. Yet parachute operations were very dangerous. Missions had to be chosen with care to give the parachutists every opportunity to attack the enemy, while at the same time preventing them from becoming hopelessly cut off. **Meticulous** planning was vital, especially for their next operation, which involved drops of thousands of parachutists in the most important airborne mission of World War II. By September 1943, the British First Airborne Division and the U.S. 82nd were on their way back to England to join the newly arrived U.S. 101st Airborne Division. Ahead lay Operation "Overlord," the Allied invasion of occupied Europe.

For the D-Day operation, the parachutists had the job of going in first to capture vital German positions and hold them until the main forces arrived. The success of the D-Day parachute landings hinged on the various units arriving at the right place at the right time. The first Allied soldiers to parachute behind the Normandy beaches, on the evening

UNDERSTAND THE FULL MEANING

meticulous: Careful, detailed, precise.

At the Battle of the Bulge, tanks and Infantrymen of the 82nd Airborne Division, Company G, 740th Tank Battalion, 504th Regiment, push through the snow toward their objective.

Parachutes open overhead as waves of paratroops land in Holland during operations by the 1st Allied Airborne Army.

of June 5, 1944, were special American teams called "pathfinders." Their job was to clear selected drop zones (DZs) of obstacles and set up "Eureka" homing beacons. In the dark, an hour behind the pathfinders, were 822 U.S. aircraft carrying more than 13,000 American paratroops.

Once over occupied territory, the pilots navigated their way across the black landscape using the faint reflections of major roads, bridges, railway lines, and rivers as reference points. Once close to the DZ, electronic receivers in the lead aircraft picked up the radio signals from the many homing beacons. As the lead C-47 aircraft crossed the coast, more than one DZ was already under attack, and many pathfinders were forced to set up their beacons under intense enemy fire.

Despite the best efforts of the pathfinders, some aircraft were still forced to drop their soldiers "blind" or on other marked DZs. Within hours, many parachutists of the 82nd and 101st Airborne Divisions had been widely scattered across France. Fifteen hundred men were injured or killed when they came down in trees, hedgerows, rivers, and farmyards. Though the operation was not going according to plan, panic and confusion swept through the German High Command as report of hundreds of separate battles filtered back from the front.

After D-Day, the two airborne divisions came together again to form a large part of Operation "Market Garden" in September 1944. This was a mission to capture German positions ahead of the Allied advance through occupied Europe. The 82nd Division had a particularly tough job. They had to capture vital bridges over the Waal at Nijmegen in Holland. The paratroops had to cross the fast-flowing river in small canvas boats. Many men died under machine-gun fire in the water. Yet the tough paras still managed to seize the northern ends of the rail and road bridges. A concerted attack on both ends of the bridge by paratroops and British tanks resulted in very bitter fighting as the Germans fought back from concealed positions among the steel girders on the bridge. Finally, at nightfall, the bridge was taken. The British Second Army's commander, General Miles Dempsey, later saluted the 82nd Airborne, referring to it as the "greatest division in the world today."

The U.S. paras fought with distinction throughout World War II. Only five years after the war ended, they were back in action in the Korean War. One parachute operation involved the paras attempting to capture a train full of U.S. prisoners. On October 22, 1950, 1,470 paratroopers and 74 tons of equipment were landed near the train route. Two days of intense fighting followed as the paras annihilated the North Korean People's Army (KPA) 239th Infantry Regiment and various other smaller units. But because bad weather had delayed the operation, the train unfortunately escaped. However, a few American survivors were rescued from a group of POWs.

After 1965, 101st Division paras were sent to a new war, in Vietnam. Vietnam was not a paratrooper's war, because the country is carpeted in jungle and it is hard to land there. The 101st launched one major airborne operation in 1967, when the paras made a drop as part of Operation "Junction City" in February 1967. The targets were **communist** bases north of Tay Ninh City. The plan involved a large parachute drop being followed up by a large helicopter assault. The

UNDERSTAND THE FULL MEANING

communist: Having to do with communism, a system in which all property is owned by the community or by the government.

assault went in on the morning of February 22 and continued until mid-May. By that time, 2,700 Viet Cong (VC) had been killed, and the VC had also lost large quantities of ammunition, medicines, and supplies, as well as over 800 tons of rice.

Ignoring enemy fire, SSG Oscar C. Gallegos, Compay B, 327th Infantry, takes careful aim with the M-72 LAW (light anti-tank weapon) during Operation "Wheeler" in Vietnam in 1967.

The Vietnam War saw a change in thinking about military parachute drops. By 1966, the 101st was turning away from parachutes to helicopters. Helicopters were in many cases better than parachutes, because they let troops move rapidly from one area of operations to another. In Vietnam,

U.S. Elites

The U.S. boasts many elite forces and some of the best soldiers in the world. In particular, the U.S. Army has the U.S. Special Forces, otherwise known as the Green Berets, so called because of the green cap worn by all soldiers of the regiment. The Special Forces were created to fight the communist guerrillas in the Vietnam War during the 1960s and 70s, and they became experts in jungle warfare. Since then, they have fought in many conflicts, including the Gulf War, and they have an excellent record of victories. The U.S. Navy has its own elite force, the U.S. Navy SEALs. The word SEAL stands for Sea, Air, and Land. It means that the SEALs will fight in any environment. Training for the SEALs is incredibly hard and few make the grade; about 80 percent fail. Those that do succeed become members of a very elite force, one that is particularly specialized in underwater and amphibious operations. Together, the Special Forces and SEALs form a powerful military force for the United States to call on in times of war and peace.

therefore, the 101st Airborne was designated "Airmobile," which meant that they could go into combat entirely in helicopters. In October 1974, the "Screaming Eagles" were officially called the 101st Airborne Division (Air Assault).

The 82nd Airborne Division also served in Vietnam. After the war, they were next used in Operation "Urgent Fury," the U.S. invasion of Grenada to rescue U.S. citizens during a time of political trouble on the island. The 82nd reinforced two Ranger battalions at Point Salines airfield. Then they moved forward to rescue American students at the True Blue Medical and Grand Anse campuses of the St. George's University Medical School. That these tasks were all accomplished within forty-eight hours says much for the 82nd Airborne's expertise as soldiers.

The first elements of the division arrived over Point Salines, on the west of the island, at midmorning. They found the eastern end of the runway still held by the enemy. As each aircraft came in to land, it attracted heavy fire, and the small runway could handle only one aircraft at a time. After a savage five-hour battle, the Rangers and 82nd Airborne secured the airfield and were finally able to reach the medical school campus by nightfall. Other students were located and evacuated during the following day.

U.S. airborne forces were the first units to be **deployed** to Saudi Arabia during Operation "Desert Shield." Desert Shield was in response to the invasion of tiny Kuwait by Iraq in August 1990. During the whole of that month, Galaxy and Starlifter aircraft flew the 82nd Airborne Division and

UNDERSTAND THE FULL MEANING

deployed: Sent into the field and positioned to be ready for combat.

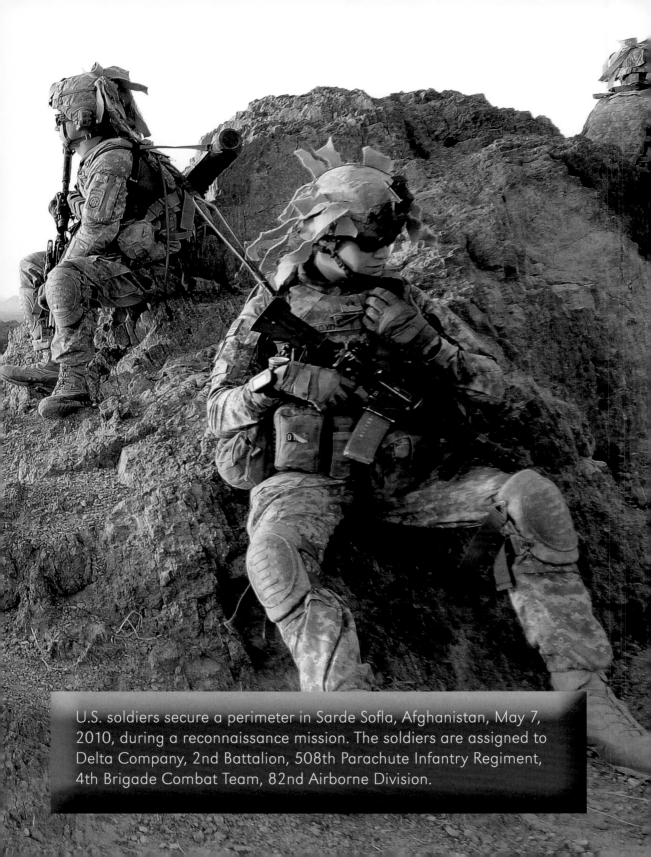

U.S. soldiers secure a perimeter in Sarde Sofla, Afghanistan, May 7, 2010, during a reconnaissance mission. The soldiers are assigned to Delta Company, 2nd Battalion, 508th Parachute Infantry Regiment, 4th Brigade Combat Team, 82nd Airborne Division.

all its equipment to Saudi Arabia, Kuwait's neighbor. In September, ships carrying the 101st Airborne Division's equipment and 350 helicopters arrived in the country. Both these divisions were secretly moved west along Iraq's undefended border.

On February 23, 1991, the Allied mission to free Kuwait began. Allied troops leapfrogged by air and land into Iraq. They established large fuel and supply dumps deep inside enemy territory. The helicopters of the 101st Division raced north and quickly seized the important town of Al Nasiriya. The Allies then swung east, destroying the elite Iraqi Republican Guard and other Iraqi units in a series of short battles. Kuwait was liberated by February 25, and the Americans called a ceasefire on the 27th. Operation "Desert Storm" had been a resounding success, in large part because of the efforts of U.S. airborne forces.

The 82nd and 101st Airborne divisions have served proudly in both the wars in Afghanistan and Iraq. In fact, these Airborne soldiers were some of the first boots on the ground in both conflicts. They dealt a decisive blow to the Afghan Taliban in 2001 and 2002 at the outset of combat operations in Afghanistan, and they were deployed to Kuwait before the U.S. invasion of Iraq in 2002 and 2003. Since the beginning of both of America's most recent wars, U.S. Airborne forces have deployed several times to Iraq and Afghanistan, called to duty when needed. As a matter of pride, almost all the division's troops are parachute trained and wear the maroon beret and "Airborne" shoulder tab, as well as the very distinctive "All American" shoulder flash.

CHAPTER 3

The Israeli Parachute Corps

Israel's airborne troops have been involved in some of the most savage battles since World War II. Though many Israeli units are expert, the Israeli paras have proved themselves to be an elite of world-class standard.

The Israeli Parachute Corps can claim to be descended from a handful of brave Jewish fighters who parachuted into occupied Europe in 1945 during World War II. Jews were being horribly persecuted and murdered by the Germans during what is today called the Holocaust. A special group of Romanian and Hungarian Jews were recruited to establish a secret escape route for Jews and also for British pilots shot down over German territory. Many of these **intrepid**

UNDERSTAND THE FULL MEANING

intrepid: Brave and daring.

units were captured and either shot or sent to prison camps. One man, Yoel Palgi, escaped from the train taking him to a concentration camp. He made his way back to Palestine. Three years later, he was given the task of forming the Israeli Parachute Corps.

By 1948, war in Palestine had become increasingly likely. The Jews in the Middle East were arguing with their Arab neighbors over the creation of a Jewish homeland on the same territory as Palestine. The British were at that time occupying Palestine. But on May 14, 1948, they withdrew and President David Ben-Gurion proclaimed the State of Israel. Fighting broke out immediately. As the fighting intensified, Ben-Gurion created the first parachute unit on May 26 as part of his vision of a range of elite units that would defend Israel.

Equipped with only a single Curtiss C-46 Commando aircraft, a small supply of parachutes, and the old RAF base at Ramat David, Major Palgi was expected to produce a company of fully trained paratroops. A core of Palgi's hundred-odd recruits consisted of Pal'mach fighters (a guerrilla-type force established in World War II by the British and the Jews to operate behind German lines if the latter's army ever invaded Palestine). However, because Jews from all over the world had come to Israel, recruits were supplemented by a mixture of French Foreign Legionnaires, American paras, and concentration camp victims. The new unit spoke more than a dozen languages and they had little new equipment or aircraft. Yet while Israel fought for its independence, the paras trained themselves into a tough unit ready for the battles of the future.

Pal'mach fighters, shown here in training for urban warfare situations, were prepared for unconventional, guerrilla situations.

Paratroopers' ability to literally fall from the sky gives them tactical advantages during major battles .

By the end of the 1940s, Israel had defeated the Arab armies. Yet the Palestinian Arabs bravely fought on with a guerrilla war. So the paratroops were expanded and turned into an elite force. For the next twenty years, they were fought in many operations against the Arabs. They launched daring raids deep behind enemy lines, taking the enemy by surprise and inflicting heavy losses on them. One of the biggest operations was in 1967 during a conflict called the Six-Day War. During this war, Israel launched a massive attack on its Arab neighbors. The paras were involved in some terrible battles and suffered many casualties. However, they came out of the conflict even more respected by the military forces of the world.

One of the biggest para battles occurred in 1973. During that year, Syria and Egypt launched an **offensive** against Israel on October 6 (the beginning of the Yom Kippur War). In response, the paras were quickly flown to the battlefield to block Egyptian tanks. One brigade found itself holding the Mitla and Jiddi Passes, while another brigade was fighting on a mountain called Mount Hermo, on the Syrian border.

The paras holding the passes were fighting a daring battle. They launched an attack across the Suez Canal on October 16. The paras crossed the canal in rubber boots under storms of bullets and shells. Once they had crossed, they had to dig in and wait for the main forces on the other side of the canal to get to them. However, by now the Egyptian troops

UNDERSTAND THE FULL MEANING

offensive: An attack.

had blocked all the approach roads to the canal. The situation was looking dangerous for the paras. But their fellow paras of the 202nd Brigade were coming to the rescue. The 202nd Brigade attacked an Egyptian base that was helping the attack on the paras at the canal. It was horrifying battle. First artillery and then tank and heavy machine-gun fire were used against the paras. A survivor later reported that the shells hurtled in as fast as machine-gun fire. Eventually, paratroops and Israeli tanks pushed through to the canal. At the canal, artillery strikes were followed by air attacks, helicopter assaults, and finally raids by Egyptian **commandos**. Nevertheless, the war ended with the Israelis still holding on to the corner of the African continent to which they had laid claim.

However, just days before the battle at the canal ended, one vital position still remained to be recaptured: Mount Hermon. During the Six-Day War, Israeli troops had built a radar station and fort on the lower slopes of the mountain. Yet Syria now held the summit, and it attacked the radar station with its own elite paras. The Israeli defenders held out all afternoon. Just as the sun was setting, a group of Syrian commandos finally scaled the walls with ropes and grappling hooks and poured into the underground chambers to end the siege.

The fort remained in Syrian hands, even though Israeli infantry threw themselves hard into a counterattack. With

UNDERSTAND THE FULL MEANING

commandos: Soldiers who are serve in units that are especially trained to act quickly and aggressively, often using guerrilla warfare tactics.

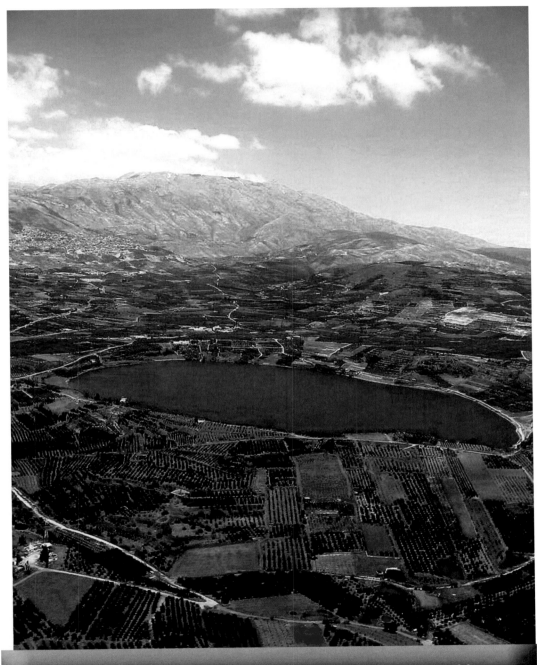

Mount Hermon is a peaceful site today, but it was the scene of fierce fighting in October 1973.

the time of the cease-fire approaching, the radar station looked likely to remain under Arab control. On October 21, the Israelis launched a last-ditch counterattack, landing a paratroop brigade on the summit of the mountain, while infantry stormed the fort positions from below. The Arab commandos fought back valiantly, knocking out most of the Israeli tanks. Despite being trapped between the paras and infantry, the Syrians held out throughout the night. Finally, at ten the next morning, a short time before the cease-fire was due to happen, the Israeli paras and infantry stepped up their attack and overwhelmed the defenders.

Another type of elite unit in Israel was connected with the Parachute Corps. These were the "Sayeret" units, formed to conduct long-range patrols and undercover operations along Israel's borders and behind enemy lines. There were various and different Sayeret groups. One of them, "Sayeret Mat'kal," is still among the world's most elite counterterrorist units.

Israel's most daring international operation using a Sayeret unit was the rescue of the passengers from an Air France airliner in 1976. The Airbus aircraft was hijacked by terrorists on June 27 and flown to Entebbe airport in Uganda, Africa. Once on the ground, the hostages were guarded by terrorists and Ugandan soldiers; rescue seemed impossible. In the early hours of July 4, four aircraft landed at Entebbe carrying a Sayeret Mat'kal hostage-rescue unit, some Israeli paras, and the elite Golani infantry brigades. In an incredible operation, the Sayeret Mat'kal soldiers rescued all the hostages, killing thirteen terrorists at the cost of only one man. While they were doing this, the infantry and paras blocked Ugandan soldiers from helping the terrorists. The entire operation was completed in 53 minutes.

Israeli paratroopers are among the world's best soldiers. In the modern era, their skills have to be kept sharp all the time due to the regularity with which they are called to secure the Israeli borders. Today's Paratroops wear the standard Israeli uniform with a maroon beret and silver parachute wings on the left breast.

CHAPTER 4
Spetsnaz

Highly secretive and deadly, for many years the Soviet Union didn't even acknowledge that the Spetsnaz units existed. These troops were trained to do a wide variety of special missions.

The Spetsnaz are the elite soldiers of Russia and the former Soviet Union. They receive training in many different types of elite operations. These include intelligence gathering, long-range reconnaissance patrols, taking hostages, attacking abroad, supporting guerrilla fighters, sabotage, and assassinations.

UNDERSTAND THE FULL MEANING

intelligence: Information, especially secret information, about what an enemy or other group is doing.

reconnaissance: Exploration for the purpose of gathering information.

The first recorded use of special forces by the Soviets occurred soon after the Russian Revolution. Small elite units were created to subdue those who did not want the communist regime. They did this with such success that more elite units were created. The Soviets also pioneered the use of airborne special forces. Reconnaissance teams, formed in 1927, were used in 1929 against Afghan **insurgents**, as well as in Central Asia. By 1932, the regular airborne forces had become almost completely dedicated to deep reconnaissance and to the destruction of the enemy's command-and-control facilities.

By the early 1930s, Soviet special operations units had largely crushed the majority of domestic dissent and felt ready to concentrate on directing their attention against anti-Soviet activity abroad. In 1936, the government created an Administration for Special Tasks to implement the ruthless elimination of its enemies abroad. During the Spanish Civil War (1936–39), for example, the newly formed People's Commissariat of Internal Affairs—which became the KGB—and the Main Intelligence Directorate of the General Staff undertook terrorist, sabotage, and guerrilla activities behind nationalist lines on a scale never before envisioned.

World War II saw the creation of many more of the Soviet elite forces. They played a crucial part in the ultimate Soviet victory and fought in some of the most hostile environments

UNDERSTAND THE FULL MEANING

insurgents: Rebels; people who rise up against the established government.

stamina: Endurance; the ability to keep going through difficulties.

imaginable, including above the Arctic Circle in northern Russia, Finland, and Norway, and in the Soviet Far East. Special navy units were also created. These undertook aggressive search-and-destroy missions against German positions on the coast and did daring operations to snatch prisoners.

Most elite troops at this time were selected on the basis of their absolute loyalty to the Communist Party, and also their toughness and **stamina**. Most were between eighteen and thirty years old, and in many cases, they were very experienced sportsmen and hunters. Training was incredibly tough. Even in training exercises, injured and exhausted soldiers were simply left on their own without help. The same thing happened on real missions and meant that the special forces suffered a very high casualty rate.

Yet they conducted some of the most daring raids of the war. During the winter of 1942–43 alone, Special Forces groups behind the lines derailed 576 trains and five armored trains and blew up about 300 tanks, 650 other vehicles, and more than 300 rail and road bridges, killing and wounding thousands of enemy soldiers in the process.

Two particular missions stand out. In July 1943, 316 Spetsnaz were parachuted into action up to 186 miles (300 km) behind the Germans' front line. With help from local people, they laid more than 3,500 explosive charges on over 435 miles (700 km) of railway track and blew the track sky high. This mission made travel around the vast distances of Russia very difficult for the Germans. It also had the effect of making the Germans very nervous, even when they were in places that were previously thought safe.

The other mission occurred on the night of March 11, 1943. A twenty-three-man party of Spetsnaz led by Lieutenant I.P. Kovalev parachuted behind German lines in the Novorzhev area. After making contact with **partisans**, the Spetsnaz went into action on March 17. Silently and stealthily, they set about laying explosive charges on local roads and railway lines. They often worked under the very noses of German sentries. Such men must have had nerves of steel. Over the next seven months, the group sabotaged one mile (1.6 km) of telephone lines, two and a half miles (4 km) of railway track, and seventeen bridges. These actions resulted in the destruction of two tanks, eight truckloads of ammunition, several dozen vehicles, and sixteen military trains. When the partisans and commandos linked up with the Red Army

A group of Soviet Spetsnaz prepares for their mission in Afghanistan.

in October 1943, Kovalev was awarded a medal called the Hero of the Soviet Union, with the rest of the party receiving the Order of the Patriotic War or the Red Star.

After World War II, Spetsnaz forces were used in many different operations, particularly in suppressing young people who did not want to be under communist control. One of their biggest operations was when the Soviet Union invaded and occupied the country of Afghanistan in 1979. Between December 8 and December 10, 1979, some fourteen days before the invasion, Spetsnaz troops moved in to capture a vital tunnel that would be used by the main Soviet invasion. Then the Spetsnaz captured Kabul International Airport (Kabul is the capital of Afghanistan). Over the next few days, the Spetsnaz soldiers accomplished many missions before the main invasion force arrived and took over Afghanistan in a matter of days.

But the occupation was not to be a quiet one. Afghan guerrillas—called the Mujahedeen—fought hard over the next nine years to throw the Soviet troops out of their country. That is why, in 1983, Spetsnaz forces again went on the offensive. Working from heavily armored helicopters, they attacked isolated towns and villages, which the Mujahedeen had once considered safe. Villages suspected of helping the guerrillas were burned to the ground in vicious operations. Some of these operations may have even been carried out by Spetsnaz disguised as guerrillas.

UNDERSTAND THE FULL MEANING

partisans: Members of a guerrilla group who are involved in fighting an occupying army.

In the spring of 1985, Spetsnaz troops began to fight with **conventional** units in an attempt to rid the Afghan valleys of the enemy. Helicopters would fly the Spetsnaz troops over the mountains in front of the advancing tanks to catch the unsuspecting enemy in the open. Casualties on both sides were heavy, through the Soviets appeared willing to pay this high price. As a result, the Spetsnaz soldiers became known as some of the toughest in the world. These troops were battled-hardened and excellent at mountain warfare. They quickly began to notch up successes. Reconnaissance units operated from camouflaged hides high in the mountains. Some groups were disguised as Afghan people so that they could move freely about the mountain passes. Others were dropped many miles from their targets, traveling through the night to lay ambushes and observe the Mujahedeen. The role of Spetsnaz within Afghanistan was vital. However, the constant death toll among Soviet troops in Afghanistan made the war very unpopular back at home. In 1989, all Soviet forces withdrew from the country.

The Special Operations Brigade is the basic Spetsnaz unit. Each brigade usually includes three or four parachute battalions. A Spetznaz brigade has between 1,000 and 1,300 men. It is trained to operate either as a single unit or as many smaller units.

In 1989, the forces of communism in Russia collapsed. Russia's old enemies in the West—particularly the United

UNDERSTAND THE FULL MEANING

conventional: Typical, usual; in terms of military troops, conventional is the opposite of guerrilla forces.

In the 1980s, Afghanistan's barren and mountainous terrain offered challenges to the Soviet Spetsnaz, just as it does today to U.S. forces fighting there.

The Cold War

The Cold War (1945–1989) was not really a war at all. It actually describes the hostility between the Soviet Union and the Western powers (the United States, Britain, and much of Europe) that nearly, but not quite, resulted in war. The Cold War began at the end of World War II, when Germany had been conquered by the Soviet Union from the east and Allied forces from the west. The Soviet Union held on to many of the countries it had passed through during the conflict and made them communist, a practice that the West opposed. Germany was cut in half and eventually a huge wall was built through Berlin (separating East and West Germany), with the communists on one side and the Western powers on the other. The Cold War lasted for over forty years. Both sides felt the other's way of life was dangerous. Both had nuclear weapons and made it clear that they would use them if the other side attacked. Though many wars between communism and democracy happened around the world, the two superpowers of the United States and the Soviet Union never fought each other, despite coming close on several occasions. Eventually, the Cold War ended when the old communist regime in Russia collapsed in 1989. The Berlin Wall, the last bastion of Cold War politics, was torn down, and there began a new era in world history.

States and Great Britain—became Russia's friends. Before this happened, much of the Spetsnaz training was concerned with what to do in case of a war against the United States and her allies. In the two decades since the collapse of the Soviet Union, however, Russian special forces have been combating rebels in Chechnya, terrorists abroad, and even Somali pirates. In the 1990s, Russian special forces were involved in the First and Second Chechen Wars, as Russia attempted to stem terrorist attacks launched from Chechnya and maintain Russian control of the region. In 2010, Russian special forces received worldwide attention for their rescue of a crew of an oil tanker that had been captured by pirates off the coast of Somalia.

CHAPTER 5

The British SAS

The Special Air Service is the most highly trained special forces unit in the world. Since it was created in World War II, the regiment has achieved some startling victories. Today, it is at the forefront of the fight against international terrorism.

The background to the Special Air Service (SAS) Regiment's creation was the bitter struggle in North Africa during World War II. Throughout 1941, elite German forces were pushing back the Allies. A way had to be found to strike back at the Germans, especially the weak areas behind their lines. The founder of the SAS, a British officer, David Stirling, devised a plan to parachute small teams behind enemy lines. He thought that once they were there they could attack German gasoline storage tanks and airfields, both things the Germans needed to fight the war.

Stirling's idea was given the green light, and he created the Special Air Service, at first only about sixty-four men strong. Unfortunately, the first operation was a disaster. On the night of November 18, 1941, five aircraft carrying the SAS soldiers took off on a parachute mission against some German airfields. However, they soon ran into gale-force winds and heavy rain. Two aircraft were lost and the parachutists widely scattered. No targets were attacked, and two days later, only twenty-two tired and hungry men struggled back to safety. Undaunted, Stirling still believed that parachutes were the best way to attack. He adjusted his approach, and this time they had great success. Stirling's men destroyed sixty-one aircraft and a number of vehicles. Once the SAS had learned the art of desert survival, they went on many raids in North Africa as well.

Though Stirling was eventually captured by the Germans, he had created one of the world's best units at the time. They went on to fight with amazing bravery throughout the rest of the war. While fighting in German-occupied Europe, one SAS unit alone destroyed seventy vehicles, killed 220 enemy troops, and derailed six trains. Other units became legendary. On August 22, 1944, Captain Derrick Harrison and a small SAS unit drove their Jeeps into a French town. Unexpectedly, they were met by a large force of German soldiers, many more than were in the SAS party—but in the following battle, over sixty Germans were killed.

UNDERSTAND THE FULL MEANING

liberation: The act of setting someone free.

Though they served with incredible results through World War II, the SAS was disbanded when the war ended. It was not long before they were needed again, however, this time to fight an unusual war in Malaya, a British colony in the Far East. In 1948, Malayan guerrillas launched a war of **liberation** against the British. Faced with a difficult and dangerous

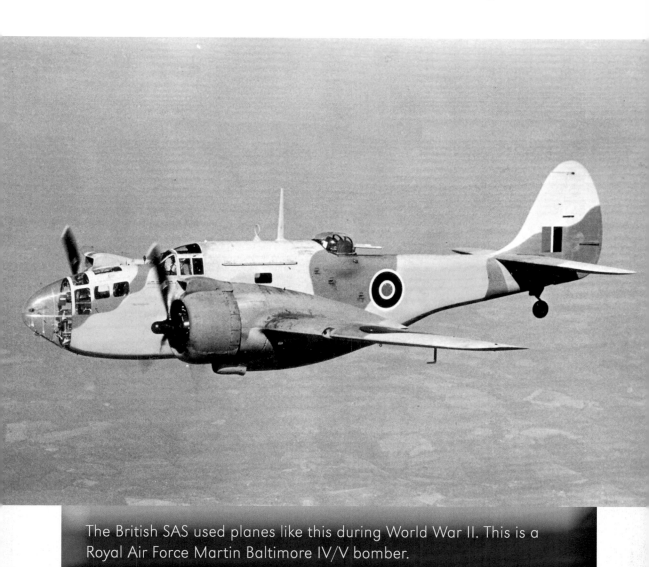

The British SAS used planes like this during World War II. This is a Royal Air Force Martin Baltimore IV/V bomber.

situation, one British officer decided that an elite unit was needed to take the war into the guerrilla **sanctuary** areas. That officer was "Mad" Mike Calvert, an experienced former SAS soldier from World War II. The unit he formed became the new SAS.

Some of the SAS work in Malaya involved operations in both the mountains and the jungle. The SAS approach relied on the use of four-man long-range reconnaissance patrols. They also made many friends among the local civilians. By doing so, they helped people support the British rather than the guerrillas. Infiltrating guerrilla-controlled areas by parachuting into the jungle, patrols gradually built up a picture of enemy activity from well-used tracks, arms dumps, and camps. This information was then later used to lay ambushes and launch search-and-destroy operations. A number of terrorist leaders were followed back to their hideouts and killed or captured by the SAS.

Malaya was only the first of many operations for the new SAS. Next stop was Borneo. This time the enemy was not guerrillas, but regular soldiers, often Indonesian paratroops and marines. The parties of soldiers crossing the long border of mountainous jungle were engaged in sabotage or terrorist missions. Two- and four-man SAS surveillance posts

UNDERSTAND THE FULL MEANING

sanctuary: A safe place, a refuge.

Commonwealth: An association of independent countries, formerly parts of the British Empire, that cooperate on issues of common interest.

were established all the way down the border to report on enemy movements. This was helped by winning the hearts and minds of the jungle tribes and then using them to gather important information as well. The SAS also embarked on highly secret operations to identify and attack enemy bases just inside Indonesian territory. SAS activities helped to win a victory for the British in Borneo when Indonesia decided it was losing too many men to this elite force. **Commonwealth** forces killed more the 2,000 Indonesians at a cost of 115 servicemen killed and around twice that number wounded. The SAS lost only three men, while two were wounded.

SAS Jungle Training

The first thing that SAS instructors do when the new recruits arrive on their jungle survival course is get them used to the jungle. For many it comes as a shock. Everything is different: the climate, the trees and plants, and the animals. During their four to six weeks in the jungle, the recruits are taught to find food and water. These things are actually quite easy to do because the jungle is bursting with life. What is difficult is avoiding the many poisonous plants and animals that live there, and also coping with many tropical diseases. Because of this, SAS soldiers are taught how to recognize dangerous wildlife and plant life and avoid it. They are also taught how to treat themselves and friends for illnesses that could be fatal in the jungle. SAS soldiers have used their jungle survival skills in places such as Malaya and Borneo.

Like Afghanistan, the land of Oman is rugged and rocky. The special skills of the British SAS were especially useful.

At the beginning of the 1970s, the SAS returned to a country in the Middle East called Oman. They had been there in the 1950s and had amazing success. Now they were faced with a large-scale guerrilla war. This was caused by a group called the People's Front for the Liberation of the Occupied Arabian Gulf (PFLOAG). It was attempting to overthrow the government of the Sultan of Oman, and Britain sent forces to help the government resist. The SAS set about creating small military units made up of the local people.

By 1974, the Sultan's 15,000-strong army was made bigger by about around 1,600 of these civilian soldiers, led by fifty to a hundred SAS soldiers. As in earlier conflicts, the SAS showed they were real experts. In one battle at a place called Mirbat, a handful of SAS soldiers held off 250 guerrillas. Nowhere was safe for the guerrillas. The successful Omani campaign cost the lives of only twelve SAS soldiers.

Between 1968 and 1974, terrorism became a new problem all over the world. This provided a new role for the SAS as a counterterrorist force. A Counter Revolutionary Warfare Wing was set up at Hereford—the SAS headquarters in England—to provide training in the techniques of counterterrorism. Special Projects Teams (SPTs) also received their training in hostage-rescue techniques.

One of the most prominent areas of SAS operations was Northern Ireland. From the late 1960s, this province of the United Kingdom had been experiencing a violent and ongoing war between two different religious communities. The British Army and government were also targets of the terrorists. The SAS went to Northern Ireland to fight the terrorists at their own game. One area of the province that received particular attention was South Armagh, known as "Bandit Country," the heartland of the chief terrorist organization. The main role of the SAS in Northern Ireland was—and still is—gathering information. But they were also used to capture high-ranking terrorists. The regiment quickly became feared and loathed by the enemy fighters.

Carrying out operations in Northern Ireland was very complex, a fact illustrated forcibly in May 1976, when the Southern Ireland police arrested two parties of the SAS after they accidentally crossed the border. There were also problems with SAS surveillance operations. In July 1978, a serious breakdown in communications between the Army and the Royal Ulster Constabulary (RUC) resulted in an SAS surveillance team accidentally killing an innocent sixteen-year-old schoolboy, when he returned to look at a secret store of arms that he had earlier discovered.

The SAS have always operated in difficult environments, and Northern Ireland was as challenging as any. But it was terrorists from a different country that brought the regiment to the attention of people around the world.

In 1980, terrorists took over the Iranian embassy in London. Then the terrorists shot dead one of their twenty-six hostages. It was time for the SAS to go into action.

As the world watched on TV, the black-clad counterterrorist soldiers, amid smoke, explosions, and gunfire, **abseiled**

UNDERSTAND THE FULL MEANING

abseiled: Rappelled; used a certain method of moving down steep surfaces by means of a rope.

down the sides of the building and entered the embassy to rescue the hostages. For many of those watching, it was the first time they had ever heard of an organization called the Special Air Service. The operation was an incredible success, with almost all the hostages rescued unhurt and all the terrorists either killed or captured. The regiment has been in the media spotlight ever since.

The Falklands War, which began in April 1982, gave the regiment an opportunity to practice other roles than simply hostage-rescue. The SAS were part of a large British force sent to recapture the Falkland Islands after Argentina invaded and occupied them. Reconnaissance teams, which spent many tense days hidden behind Argentine lines, locating, identifying, and assessing the strength of enemy forces, made a vital contribution to the success of the ground operations. However, the regiment is more likely to be remembered for the more famous raid on Pebble Island on May 15, when SAS troopers destroyed eleven enemy aircraft in a classic nighttime operation.

During the 1991 Gulf War, SAS teams were inserted deep behind enemy lines inside Iraq and Kuwait to assist Allied operations. Missions included finding important enemy targets such as Iraqi headquarters, Scud surface-to-surface missile launchers, and command bunkers. They further assisted Allied aircraft in destroying these targets by fixing them with special laser beams that controlled aircraft bombs. The beam would bounce off the target into the sky, creating a "tunnel" down which a laser-guided bomb could travel. Other operations involved rescuing and evacuating Allied aircrew who had been shot down.

The British SAS fought with American and local troops during the early days of the war against the Taliban in Afghanistan.

The SAS is currently part of U.K. Special Forces Group, which also includes the Royal Marines' Special Boat Service (formally Squadron). The SAS is based at Stirling Lines in Hereford and consists of four "Sabre" Squadrons (A, B, D, and G Squadrons) and an Army Reserve "Sabre" Squadron (R Squadron). Each squadron is divided into four troops: Mountain, Boat, Mobility, and Air Troop, each specializing in different methods of combat and different environments. Each troop consists of four four-man fighting patrols. In turn, each of these has a signaler, linguist (someone who is good at speaking foreign languages), a medic, and a **demolitions** specialist.

In the modern War on Terror, British SAS troops have helped battle the Taliban in Afghanistan in the early days of the conflict in that country. In addition, they have deployed to Iraq during the American campaign, where they served as part of the international coalition forces. To this day, the SAS remains Britain's most specialized unit and probably the world's greatest elite force. The influence of the SAS on other countries' special forces is immense. Most special forces units around the world take their inspiration from the best of the British military, the Special Air Service.

UNDERSTAND THE FULL MEANING

demolitions: Having to do with the use of explosives.

CHAPTER 6
The Australian SAS Regiment

The Australian SAS Regiment, like its British counterpart, is highly trained and superbly equipped. Formed during the 1950s, it saw extensive service in Vietnam, where it achieved much success. Many experts now rate the regiment as being among the best in the world.

Today's Australian elite units have their roots in World War II. The Imperial Japanese Army came close to Australia's shores when it invaded New Guinea and the Pacific Islands in early 1942. Across a short strip of ocean, the remote outposts of northern Australia prepared to meet the enemy with guerrilla warfare.

The Australians knew they were experts in fighting and surviving the arid bush land and deserts of their continent. So the Second/First North Australia Observer Unit was raised in July 1942 to patrol into remote, unmapped areas of the northern coast and report on enemy movements. In the event of an invasion, the "Nackeroos" were to remain behind to report on the advancing Japanese forces. Across the sea, other groups, such as the civilian Coastwatchers and M Special Force, also collected vital intelligence from behind the lines. Some special groups actually fought the Japanese, such as the Australian Independent Commando Companies and Z Special Force, who took the war into the enemy's camp.

At the end of the war, all but a few regular Australian Army infantry units were **demobilized** as the danger receded. The move toward a post-war elite airborne unit began on October 23, 1951. On this date, an airborne platoon of the Royal Australia Regiment (RAR) was created. This was intended mainly for rescue roles and was also there as a rapid-reaction force in case of national emergencies. Two commando units were also raised in 1955.

The First Australian SAS Company was created in 1957. The primary role of the new SAS unit was reconnaissance, inserting parachutists deep into enemy territory to gather intelligence. The Company was organized as a commando unit line and was based at Swanbourne Barracks, Perth (northern Australia). The men wore red berets with the crossed rifles of the Royal Australian Infantry Corps. They spent the next few years training in the hostile terrain of northwestern Australia. These exercises were not without

UNDERSTAND THE FULL MEANING

demobilized: Disbanded, stopped functioning as a group.

Modern Australian recruits wait their turn during their paratrooper training.

incident, as Lieutenant-Colonel David Horner tells us: "Two other members of the company had to abandon a twelve-foot rubber **dinghy** when a crocodile climbed aboard. Sharks were in the area, but the two men gingerly pulled up the anchor and towed the dingy ashore with the crocodile as a passenger."

The Australian SAS troops were soon fighting in Borneo alongside the British and New Zealand SAS. They proved they were excellent soldiers, and so the Australian authorities decided to expand their numbers. The new unit had a total of fifteen officers and eighty-six other ranks. For a while, the red berets were kept. However, parachute-qualified troopers were entitled to wear the distinctive SAS Sabre Squadron wings.

The Australians soon showed they were worthy of the elite name. In Borneo, they did everything that the British SAS was doing, building support among the local people and conducting dangerous combat and reconnaissance missions into the Bornean jungle. Occasionally, they were asked to lead large forces of conventional infantry back across the border to hit groups of enemy troops. Despite the increased safety in numbers, these operations often proved to be more dangerous than the reconnaissance patrols.

On January 30, 1966, a large squadron-sized force, composed of infantry and various SAS soldiers, was deployed to attack an Indonesian base on the Sekayan River, where it was believed a large enemy force was assembling for a raid

UNDERSTAND THE FULL MEANING

dinghy: A small boat.

across the border. The SAS squadron crossed the frontier unobserved. They eventually reached the river at dusk on February 3. Intending to catch the Indonesians unaware at dawn the next day, the party crossed the river and advanced along the river bank. Suddenly, the lead troops stumbled into the enemy camp and were immediately pinned down by gunfire. The situation grew worse and worse, and the units had to withdraw. Three SAS soldiers were trapped in a small

The Australian SAS are skilled at low-level flying maneuvers.

hut. To cover their withdrawal, one of the SAS soldiers threw a grenade. However, it struck an upright beam on the far side of the hut and bounced back to explode among the Australians themselves. The three men were badly wounded.

Suffering severe burns and cut off from the rest of the squadron withdrawing across the river, the plight of the men became even more desperate when artillery fire rained down on them. Once across the river, the long journey to the border became a nightmare for the badly injured soldiers. They were forced to crawl along pig trails, compasses in hand, to avoid any Indonesian survivors who might be looking for them. Reaching the border around dawn, the soldiers pressed on, finally reaching safety around mid-morning.

Later in 1966, the Australian SAS found itself involved with a new war in Vietnam. The first SAS operations concentrated on intelligence gathering and hitting small Viet Cong (VC) outposts. Soon the VC struck back in force, and there were some major battles between the Australian and Vietnamese communist forces. After battles, four- or five-man SAS patrols searched for parties of VC who had survived. Firefights were common, but the SAS almost always came out on top. In five years, the Australian and New Zealand SAS killed more than five hundred enemy soldiers for the loss of every man killed by enemy fire and twenty-seven wounded. In captured documents, the communists referred to the SAS as the Ma Rung, or "jungle ghosts." The enemy put a price on their heads, reputedly $5,000, dead or alive.

The Viet Cong patrol that resulted in a single SAS death provides a fascinating picture of these operations. On

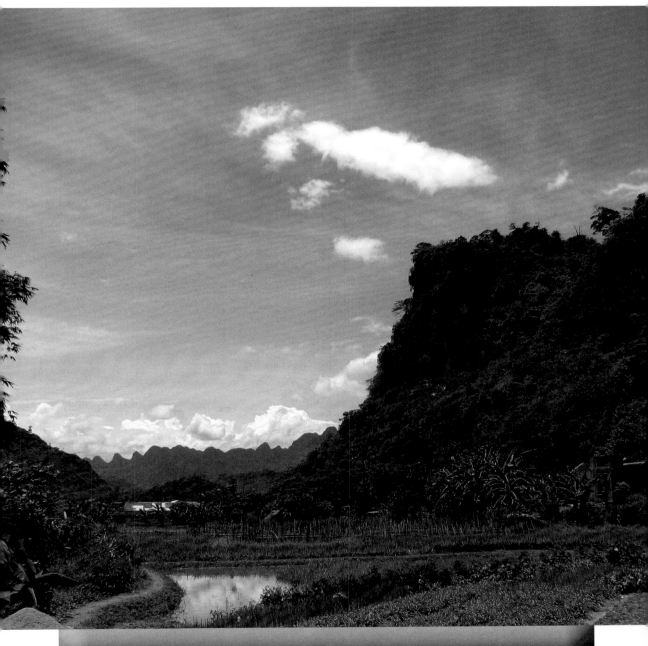

Vietnam's terrain, full of jungles and swamplands, offered the Australian SAS very different challenges from what they would face four decades later in Afghanistan.

January 17, 1967, an SAS patrol, commanded by Sergeant Norm Ferguson, was dropped by helicopter into an enemy-controlled area of open grassland and jungle. Sounds could be heard from a VC base nearby. The next morning, as the patrol began to circle the enemy camp, an ambush was sprung from the patrol's left side. Private Russell Copeman,

The Vietnam War

The Vietnam War was one of the saddest episodes in recent U. S. history. Vietnam in the early 1960s was divided into two halves. North Vietnam was communist, but South Vietnam was backed by the United States and other anti-communist countries. The North wanted to take over the South and make it communist. The United States became involved in the conflict and fought there between 1963 and 1973. The U.S. forces battled in challenging jungle conditions, and the losses started to add up. Over 58,000 U.S. soldiers were killed during the conflict. Eventually, the public at home had had enough, and the U.S. started to pull out of Vietnam in 1968. The last U.S. troops left in 1973, and South Vietnam fought on alone. In 1975, the South fell to the communists.

the patrol's medic, was hit twice by enemy fire. The patrol reacted quickly and exploded smoke grenades before disappearing back into the jungle.

However, the patrol was now hampered by the badly wounded man. It managed to just keep ahead of the enemy search parties. Over the next hour, and with the enemy in almost continual contact, the patrol stopped only briefly to dress the medic's wounds and radio for a helicopter rescue. When the RAAF helicopter appeared overhead, Copeman and another soldier were lifted aboard. But the enemy charged into the small clearing, despite a constant hail of fire from the helicopter door-gunner. The last man to be extracted was Sergeant Ferguson, who was forced to fire at a party of VC who rushed into the clearing while he was still dangling from the aircraft's **winch** rope. Sadly, Copeman died four months later from complications due to his injuries.

During Australia's ten-year involvement in Vietnam, the SAS squadrons were usually rotated on nine-month attachments to the main task force. Long-range reconnaissance patrols still formed the majority of the regiment's work, but ambushes, raids, and prisoner snatches were also undertaken. Some of the last operations included running patrols into dangerous VC sanctuary areas such as the May Taos Mountains. Other tasks included prisoner-of-war (POW) rescue operations ("Bright Light" missions) with the U.S. SEALs. The Australians finally left Vietnam in December 1972.

In the aftermath of the Vietnam War, the SAS were given two new roles inside Australia: conducting regional long-range surveillance patrols (LRSPs) in the vast northwestern deserts, and counterterrorism. The final **impetus** to create an Australian hostage-rescue/counterterrorist (HRU/CT)

UNDERSTAND THE FULL MEANING

winch: Having to do with something used for hoisting or hauling.

impetus: Action causing or inspiring another action.

Australian Light Armoured Vehicles provided security with superior firepower in Afghanistan.

force was provided by the bombing of the Hilton Hotel in Sydney on February 13, 1978. A year later, permission was given to establish the Tactical Assault Group (TAG) within SASR to provide specialist support for the Commonwealth Police.

Like other modern elite forces, the Australian SAS are now experts in fighting terrorism and rescuing hostages, as well as fighting battles on open ground. A special Training Squadron is responsible for selection and advanced training. The Australian SAS wear standard Australian Army uniforms with the distinctive sand-colored beret and the famous winged dagger SAS badge. The Australian SAS have also been involved in operations in Afghanistan since the terrorist attacks on the United States on September 11, 2001, deployed to assist international forces in combating terrorism and the Afghan Taliban.

CHAPTER 7
Weapons and Equipment

There may be many different types of elite units, but they all need to have the best military weapons and equipment available in order to carry out their high-risk missions. The most important tools of their trade are personal weapons and the transport that takes them into action, and those are the focus of this chapter.

Elite forces throughout the world use a wide variety of weapons and military equipment, ranging from handguns, submachine guns (SMGs), and automatic rifles, to air-portable vehicles, specialized aircraft, and high-speed assault craft.

Special forces units undertake a wide range of operations that are notably different from those of conventional infantry forces. The latter are trained to operate on the battlefield as components of a large military machine and are supported by armor, artillery, helicopters, and aircraft. Special forces, by comparison, often fight as small-sized, unsupported teams deep behind enemy lines. All team members must be highly proficient in the use of their individual weapons, but the weapons themselves, to serve them in their mission, must also fulfill certain criteria.

ABSOLUTE RELIABILITY

Since special forces missions often involve short, violent contacts with the enemy, a reliable weapon is essential. Weapons must work the first time and every time. A Spetsnaz team using new AN-94 Abakan rifles, for example, knows they can always be relied upon even when caked in mud or covered in snow. Similarly, SAS hostage-rescue units (HRUs) know their MP5 series submachine guns (SMGs) will always work every time during a siege-busting operation.

WEIGHT

Since many special forces missions are conducted on foot and over difficult terrain, individual weapons must be as light as possible. Weight is of even more importance to elite airborne troops, who are required to manhandle their equipment into combat. Meanwhile, the trend over the last sixty years has been toward heavier assault rifles, a consequence of the increasing complexity of internal working parts. The .303 Lee Enfield weighs 9 pounds (4.1 kg) loaded, compared

A soldier from the 34th Hungarian Special Forces Battalion fires a Glock pistol during weapons training.

to 9.5 pounds (4.3 kg) for the 7.62-millimeter L1A1 Self-Loading Rifle (SLR), 8 pounds (3.6 kg) for the Soviet 5.45-millimeter AK-74, and 11 pounds (4.98 kg) for the new British 5.56-millimeter L85A1 (SA-80). The increased use of plastics in the construction of weapons, especially in the Heckler & Koch G11, the SA-80, and the innovative Glock range of handguns, seems set to reverse this trend. Though the overall weight of the infantry rifle has increased since World War II, the change to smaller **caliber** ammunition means that individual rounds weigh less than their **predecessors**, enabling more to be carried by individual soldiers.

SIZE

The length of a weapon determines its **maneuverability** and the ease with which it can be fired from the range of positions (sitting, prone, shoulder, or hip) essential for special forces work. With the exception of the L1A1, later rifles have been shorter than the old Lee Enfield: Lee Enfield (45 in, 113 cm), L1A1 (46 in, 114 cm), M16A2 (38 in, 94 cm), and SA-80 (31 in, 78.5 cm). The MP5K series used by SAS and other HRUs is only 13 inches (32.5 cm) long.

UNDERSTAND THE FULL MEANING

caliber: The diameter of the barrel of a gun, indicating the size of the ammunition.

predecessors: Those that came before.

maneuverability: Having to do with the ease of moving something.

A U.S. Soldier from the 1st Battalion, 10th Special Forces Group fires an M-249 squad automatic weapon during weapons training.

A Special Forces soldier fires an M2, 50 caliber heavy-barrel machine

MAXIMUM FIREPOWER

The 1980s witnessed the introduction into service of a number of weapons that had smaller calibers than their predecessors, such as the SA-80 that replaced the SLR, and the AK-74 that replaced the AK-47. The smaller 5.56-millimeter cartridge resulted in an overall reduction in weapon size and **recoil**.

In addition, the rounds displayed an increased **lethality** when compared to the older and heavier 7.62-millimeter bullets, because they "tumbled" rapidly when they hit the target, and delivered their energy in a massive fashion rather that passing through the target with minimal **energy transfer**. This latter problem is especially true of the standard nine-millimeter round, which has a tendency to pass straight through the body of a victim and keep on going. FBI files, for example, contain documented cases where felons were hit with between 30 to 40 nine-millimeter bullets during the course of long firefights and still continued to fight, and even kill several officers, before themselves receiving a mortal wound!

UNDERSTAND THE FULL MEANING

recoil: The distance a weapon moves backward after it is fired.

lethality: A measure of how deadly something is.

energy transfer: The movement of energy from one thing to another. When a bullet transfers its energy to what it has hit, the power built up as the bullet has sped from the weapon is passed to its target and that energy then creates a shockwave within the target.

But while the weapons elite soldiers carry in their armory are vital to the successful completion of missions, without effective transport they will not reach their location in the first place. Transportation to and from a mission has always presented difficulties for commanders throughout history, and this is especially true of special forces and airborne units. Secret methods of going behind enemy lines are essential for units such as the SAS; discovery can mean death or capture. Specialized high-altitude, low-opening (HALO) parachute techniques let soldiers be dropped from heights of about 32,000 feet (10,000 m) and descend silently to their drop zone (DZ) undetected. They open their parachutes only at the last minute before floating a short distance to earth. Similarly, high-altitude, high-opening (HAHO) parachute methods, where the soldiers open their parachutes immediately after leaving the aircraft, are also used by special forces. The HAHO technique lets soldiers "fly" their parachutes up to 50 miles (80 km) before touching down, making it an ideal silent insertion method.

The aircraft used by special forces for parachute drops are also employed by conventional airborne units. Formations such as the British and Israeli paras, as well as the U.S. 82nd Airborne Division, employ so-called static-line parachuting (in which the soldier's parachutes open automatically as they leave the aircraft) as opposed to freefall techniques. The aircraft used include the Lockheed C-130 Hercules. This is a four-engined aircraft with a range of 2,500 miles (4,000 km)

UNDERSTAND THE FULL MEANING

fuselage: The central body of an aircraft.

and the capacity to carry sixty-five paratroopers. The giant American C-141 Starlifter can transport 155 paratroopers in its **fuselage**. Russia, too, has a large airlift capability. It has over 600 Il-76 Candid heavy-transport aircraft, each capable of carrying 140 paratroopers.

The helicopter is an ideal, if expensive, tool for special forces operations. No other military vehicle can match its speed and cross-country mobility. A number of helicopters

Helicopters play an important role in Special Forces' efforts in Afghanistan.

are ideally suited for special forces use. The large CH-47 Chinook transport can carry 44 troops and was used in 1991 by the U.S. Marines in the Gulf War. It was also used to insert SAS and SEAL teams into Iraq and Kuwait. The American Sikorsky Corporation produces a number of helicopter models, which are in service with the U.S. Marines and other American airborne units. Their UH-60 Black Hawk assault and transport helicopter is the workhorse of the 101st Airborne Division. Capable of carrying eleven fully equipped soldiers, it can also be armed with machine guns and Hellfire antitank missiles.

Specialized land vehicles have, since World War II, played an important part in transporting special forces. The SAS patrols in the North African desert demanded rugged vehicles that could carry large quantities of food, water ammunition, and fuel, as well as people. Today, this tradition is continued with such vehicles as Land Rover's series of long-range reconnaissance vehicles, the French ACMAT VLRA, and Israeli M-325 Command Car. Vehicles such as the Land Rover are equipped with machine guns, ammunition containers, radios, smoke grenades, and camouflage netting, and have ranges in excess of 498 miles (800 km).

Another wheeled vehicle that has enjoyed great success with the American military is the High Mobility Multi-Purpose Wheeled Vehicle (HMMWV), or "Hummer." The vehicle's light aluminum body makes it ideal for transportation in the fuselage of a transport aircraft or slung underneath a helicopter; two can be carried by a Chinook, one by a Black Hawk, and up to fifteen in the fuselage of a C-5 Galaxy aircraft.

The revolutionary dune-buggy type vehicle employed by American and British special forces has a number of advantages over larger vehicles such as the Jeep and Land Rover. It is easier to conceal and to transport by air, it is more nimble, and it presents a smaller target to the enemy. Models such as the Chenowth Fast Attack Vehicle (FAV), the Wesses Saker, and Longline's Light Strike Vehicle (LSV) have power-

U.S. Navy SEALs Underwater Equipment

The U.S. Navy SEALs have an amazing variety of equipment to perform their underwater missions. When they are on diving operations, they use special breathing apparatus that does not release clouds of bubbles when the wearer exhales. This is important, as it stops sentries on ships or on shore spotting clouds of bubbles that tell them there is a diver below. The SEALs also use what are called special delivery vehicles. These are like miniature submarines. The SEAL diver sits in one and drives it underwater to his target. Once there, the diver can stick explosive charges to the bottom of a boat, or abandon the craft and head inshore. These are just two of the items that help the SEALs do their job expertly. Other equipment used by the SEALs include: the seven-person inflatable boat, handheld sonar and underwater communication devices, and various types of parachute for land and water jumps.

ful engines and can mount a variety of weapons, including machine guns, canons, and anti-tank missiles. Such vehicles were used to great effect in the Gulf War by SAS and SEAL teams to hit targets behind Iraqi lines.

U.S. Marines from Special Purpose Marine Air Ground Task Force 24

Insertion onto an enemy coastline has long been practiced by elite forces, from small teams of the British Special Boat Squadron and American SEALs, to full-scale invasions such as at D-Day and Iwo Jima in World War II. The U.S. Navy currently operates somewhere around thirty **amphibious** vehicles, down from a high of around sixty-five during the Cold War.

Both the United States and Russia also employ numerous hover craft and landing craft air cushion (LCAC) vessels. The latter are able to carry a variety of cargo, including main battle tanks, and can reach high speeds. These craft have a number of advantages over traditional ships. They have higher speeds, the ability to travel over water and flat land, and they can carry a lot of equipment. Other smaller vessels used by special forces include the two-person Klepper canoe deployed by the Special Boat Service (SBS) and various inflatable commando craft. One of these is the sub-skimmer made by Submarine Products Ltd. Sixteen feet (5 m) long and capable of a surface speed of 27 knots, this craft can convert to a mini-submarine and carry up to four divers.

Elite units have earned their fame in battle by the careful selection of the soldier, weapons and equipment, and through the unit's tactics. Training and combat bring these various elements into an effective fighting force. Highly specialized roles, such as participation in covert (secret) operations, require an even higher degree of selection and training. Competitions and exercises, held by units such

UNDERSTAND THE FULL MEANING
amphibious: Able to be used both on land and in water.

as the Royal Marines and British Parachute Regiment, put great emphasis on effective shooting after completing long, exhausting endurance marches.

Surprise and speed are essential to the commando and airborne roles, and night shooting is vital for such units as the British Special Air Service and Navy SEALs. Foreign weapon training is another essential skill for members of the special forces. Because they operate so far from base, it is likely that special forces soldiers will run out of ammunition for their own weapons and have to use the enemy's. In the closing stages of the Arnhem Battle during World War II, for example, isolated areas of the airborne perimeter were held only because British paratroops fought with captured weapons and ammunition. Firearms training is particularly intense for counterterrorist units.

However, marksmanship and good equipment in themselves do not win battles or rescue hostages; self-discipline and teamwork are also important. Many elite unit actions are won by personal courage and standards, not just the tools of war.

FIND OUT MORE ON THE INTERNET

82nd Airborne www.bragg.army.mil/82dv/History.htm

101st Airborne www.campbell.army.mil/units/101st/

Australian Army www.army.gov.au

The British Army www.army.mod.uk

Israeli Defense Force dover.idf.il/IDF/English/

SAS Information www.whodareswin.com

U.S. Army www.army.mil

The websites listed on this page were active at the time of publication. The publisher is not responsible for websites that have changed their address or discontinued operation since the date of publication. The publisher will review and update the websites upon each reprint.

FURTHER READING

Bryant, Susan. *Screaming Eagles: 101st Airborne Division.* St. Paul, Minn.: Zenith Press, 2007.

Cawthorne, Nigel. *Special Forces: War on Terror.* London, UK: John Blake Publishing, 2009.

Day, Thomas L. *Along the Tigris: The 101st Airborne Division in Operation Iraqi Freedom: February 2003 to March 2004.* New York: Schiffer Publishing, 2007.

Horner, David. *In Action with the SAS.* Crows Nest, New South Wales, Australia: Allen & Unwin, 2009.

McKay, Gary. *On Patrol with the SAS: Sleeping with Your Ears Open.* Crows Nest, New South Wales, Australia: Allen & Unwin, 2007.

McManners, Hugh. *Ultimate Special Forces.* New York: DK Adult, 2006.

McNab, Chris. *The SAS Training Manual.* London, UK: Amber Books, 2002.

Nordyke, Phil. *All American, All the Way: The Combat History of the 82nd Airborne Division in World War II.* St. Paul, Minn.: Zenith Press, 2005.

O'Farrell, Terry. *Behind Enemy Lines: An Australian SAS Soldier in Vietnam.* Crows Nest, New South Wales, Australia: Allen & Unwin, 2001.

Pushies, Fred J. *82nd Airborne.* Minneapolis, Minn.: Zenith Press, 2008.

Ryan, Mike. *The Operators: Inside the World's Special Forces.* New York: Skyhorse Publishing, 2008.

Zinsmeister, Karl. *Boots on the Ground: A Month with the 82nd Airborne in the Battle for Iraq.* New York: St. Martin's Press, 2004.

BIBILIOGRAPHY

GlobalSecurity.org. "First Chechnya War," www.globalsecurity.org/military/world/war/chechnya1.htm (2 June 2010).

GlobalSecurity.org. "Israel—55th Brigade: T'zanhanim (Paratroopers) Infantry Brigade," www.globalsecurity.org/military/world/israel/55th_brigade_tzanhanim.htm (4 June 2010).

GlobalSecurity.org. "Second Chechnya War," www.globalsecurity.org/military/world/war/chechnya2.htm (2 June 2010).

Halpin, Tony. "Russian Special Forces Storm Oil Tanker, Arrest Somali Pirates." *Times Online*, www.timesonline.co.uk/tol/news/world/africa/article7117736.ece (3 June 2010).

McNab, Chris. *The World's Best Soldiers*. Broomall, Penn.: Mason Crest Publishers, 2003.

U.S. Army. "101st Airborne Division." *The Official Homepage of Fort Campbell*, KY, www.campbell.army.mil/units/101st/ (4 June 2010).

U.S. Army. "Brief History of the 82nd Airborne Division." *Fort Bragg: Home of the Airborne and Special Operations Forces*, www.bragg.army.mil/82dv/History.htm (3 June 2010).

Who Dares Wins. "SASR: The Australian Special Air Service Regiment." *Who Dares Wins: International Special Forces Information*, www.whodareswins.com/australian-special-air-service-regiment.html (3 June 2010).

INDEX

PICTURE CREDITS

Australian Government Department of Defence: pp. 62, 67, 69, 74
Creative Commons: pp. 32, 39, 58
Elite UK Forces: p. 52
Military Photos: p. 42
U.S. Airforce: p. 55
U.S. Army: pp. 20, 23, 27, 79, 81, 85
U.S. Department of Defense: pp. 30, 36, 49, 76
U.S. Navy: pp. 8, 62, 88
U.S. National Archives: p. 24

To the best knowledge of the publisher, all images not specifically credited are in the public domain. If any image has been inadvertently uncredited, please notify Harding House Publishing Service, 220 Front Street, Vestal, New York 13850, so that credit can be given in future printings.

ABOUT THE AUTHOR

C.F. Earl is a writer living and working in Binghamton, New York. Earl writes mostly on social and historical topics, including health, the military, and finances, among other topics. An avid student of the world around him, and particularly fascinated with almost any current issue, C.F. Earl hopes to continue to write for books, websites, and other publications for as long as he is able.

ABOUT THE CONSULTANT

Colonel John Carney, Jr. is USAF-Retired, President and the CEO of the Special Operations Warrior Foundation.